The Runaway Latkes

WRITTEN BY

Leslie Kimmelman

ILLUSTRATED BY

Paul Yalowitz

ALBERT WHITMAN & COMPANY

MORTON GROVE, ILLINOIS

To the Abramowitz clan, great latke-noshers all—
without whom Hanukkah wouldn't be the same.
—L.K.

To Andrew J. Yalowitz, my newest nephew.
—P.Y.

Library of Congress Cataloging-in-Publication Data

Kimmelman, Leslie.

The runaway latkes / by Leslie Kimmelman ; illustrated by Paul Yalowitz.

p. cm.

Summary: When three potato latkes escape Rebecca Bloom's frying pan on the
first night of Hanukkah, everyone including the cantor, the rabbi, and the mayor joins in the chase.

ISBN 0-8075-7176-8

[1. Hanukkah—Fiction. 2. Jews—Fiction.] I. Yalowitz, Paul, ill. II. Title.

PZ7.K56493 Ru 2000

[E]—dc21

99-050900

Published in 2000 by Albert Whitman & Company,

6340 Oakton Street, Morton Grove, Illinois 60053-2723.

Published simultaneously in Canada by General Publishing, Limited, Toronto.

Printed in the United States of America.

10 9 8 7 6 5 4 3 2

The design is by Scott Piehl.

Note

Over two thousand years ago in ancient Judea (roughly present-day Israel), a group of Jews led by Judah Maccabee fought King Antiochus of Syria for the right to practice their religion freely. The holiday of Hanukkah celebrates the Maccabees' victory.

It also celebrates the miracle that followed the victory: inside the ancient Temple in Jerusalem, one day's lamp oil burned brightly for eight days and nights. Today, Hanukkah latkes are cooked in oil to commemorate that miracle.

The first night of Hanukkah was just a few hours away.

Rebecca Bloom was at synagogue, making potato pancakes—latkes—for the big Hanukkah party. Everyone agreed that Rebecca made the crispiest, tastiest, perfectly roundest latkes in town.

Plop! Plop! She dropped each latke in a big pan of hot oil. *Sizzle, flip. Sizzle, flip.* As she cooked, she sang to herself:

Big and round, crisp and brown,
I fry latkes by the pound!

Rebecca had just finished her first panful of latkes when, to her amazement, one, two, three latkes jumped from the oil right onto the floor! They rolled out the kitchen door, singing:

Big and round, crisp and brown,
off we roll to see the town!
And YOU can't catch us!

"Oh, my!" exclaimed Rebecca. "We need these latkes for our party tonight. Stop, latkes, stop!" But the latkes did not stop. They repeated:

Big and round, crisp and brown,
off we roll to see the town!
And YOU can't catch us!

So Rebecca turned off the stove, grabbed a tray, and ran after the latkes.

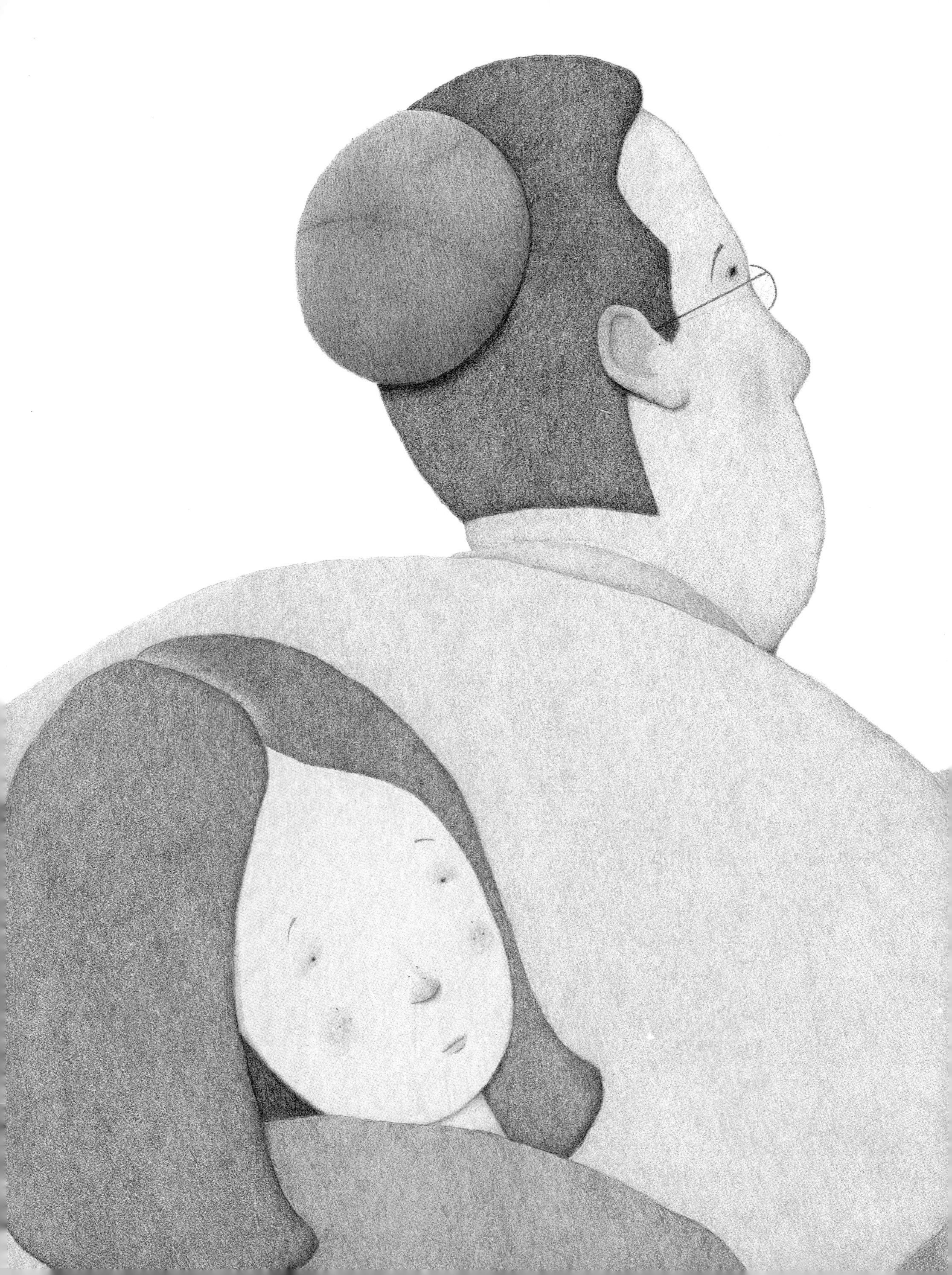

The latkes rolled along, past the door to the rabbi's study. When the rabbi saw them, he closed his book and called out, "Stop, latkes, stop! We need you for our party tonight!" But the latkes did not stop. They sang:

Big and round, crisp and brown,
off we roll to see the town!
And YOU can't catch us!

So the rabbi chased the latkes, and Rebecca chased him.

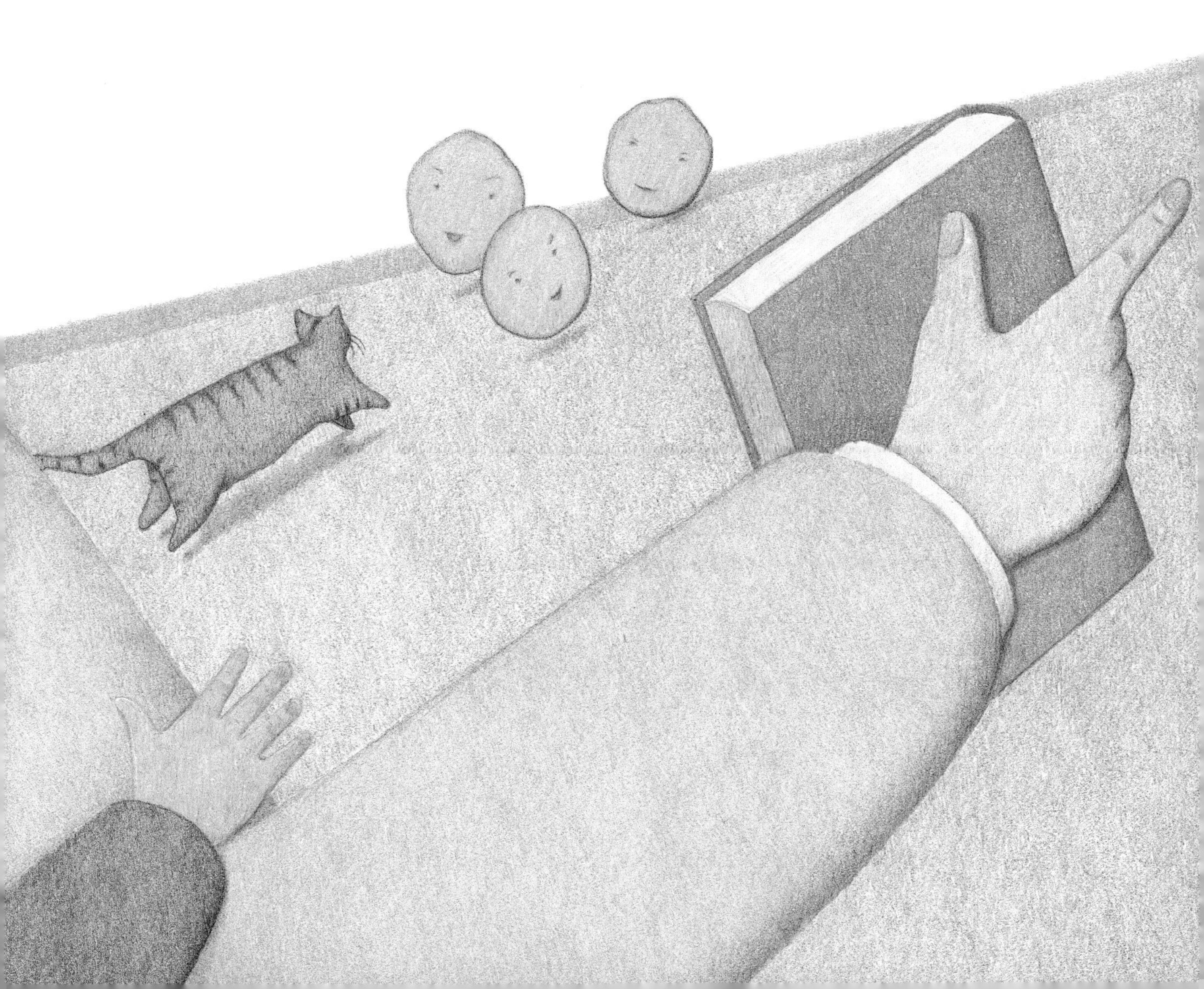

The latkes rolled along, past the room where the cantor was practicing scales. When she saw what was happening, she changed her tune.

"Stop, latkes, stop!" she trilled in a sweet voice. "We need you for our party tonight!" But the latkes did not stop. They sang:

Big and round, crisp and brown,
off we roll to see the town!
And YOU can't catch us!

So the cantor chased the latkes, and the rabbi chased the cantor, and Rebecca chased the rabbi.

The latkes rolled along, out the front door of the synagogue. Two boys were playing ball, waiting for the celebration to begin. When they saw the runaway latkes, they stopped throwing the ball to each other and threw it at the latkes instead, trying to knock them over.

"Stop, latkes, stop!" they shouted. "We want to eat you at the party tonight!" But the latkes did not stop. They sang:

Big and round, crisp and brown,
off we roll to see the town!
And YOU can't catch us!

So the boys chased the latkes, and the cantor chased the boys, and the rabbi chased the cantor, and Rebecca chased the rabbi.

CITY HALL

Through the town the latkes went. They rolled up to the mayor's office. Out he hurried to see what all the noise was about.

"Latkes!" he said. "My mother used to make latkes for me every Hanukkah!" Rubbing his stomach, he proclaimed loudly, "Stop, latkes, stop! By order of the mayor!" But the latkes did not stop. They sang:

Big and round, crisp and brown,
off we roll to see the town!
And YOU can't catch us!

So the mayor chased the latkes, and the boys chased the mayor, and the cantor chased the boys, and the rabbi chased the cantor, and Rebecca chased the rabbi.

The latkes rolled down the sidewalk in front of the police station where Sue and her partner, Harry, were just getting off for the day.

"What's that?" asked Sue. "Looks like trouble."

"Not trouble—latkes!" answered Harry, licking his lips. "Let's take 'em in for questioning!"

"Stop, latkes, stop!" Sue called out. "Stop in the name of the law!"

And Harry murmured, "Stop in the name of my empty belly!"

But the latkes did not stop. They sang:

Big and round, crisp and brown,
off we roll to see the town!
And YOU can't catch us!

Now after all this rolling, the latkes were hot—even hotter than they had been in Rebecca Bloom's frying pan. Just ahead of them, at the edge of town, was a cool, wide river called Applesauce River. The latkes rolled straight toward it.

"No!" cried the police officers and the mayor and the boys and the cantor and the rabbi and Rebecca. "Stop! You'll get wet and soggy. Then no one will be able to eat you."

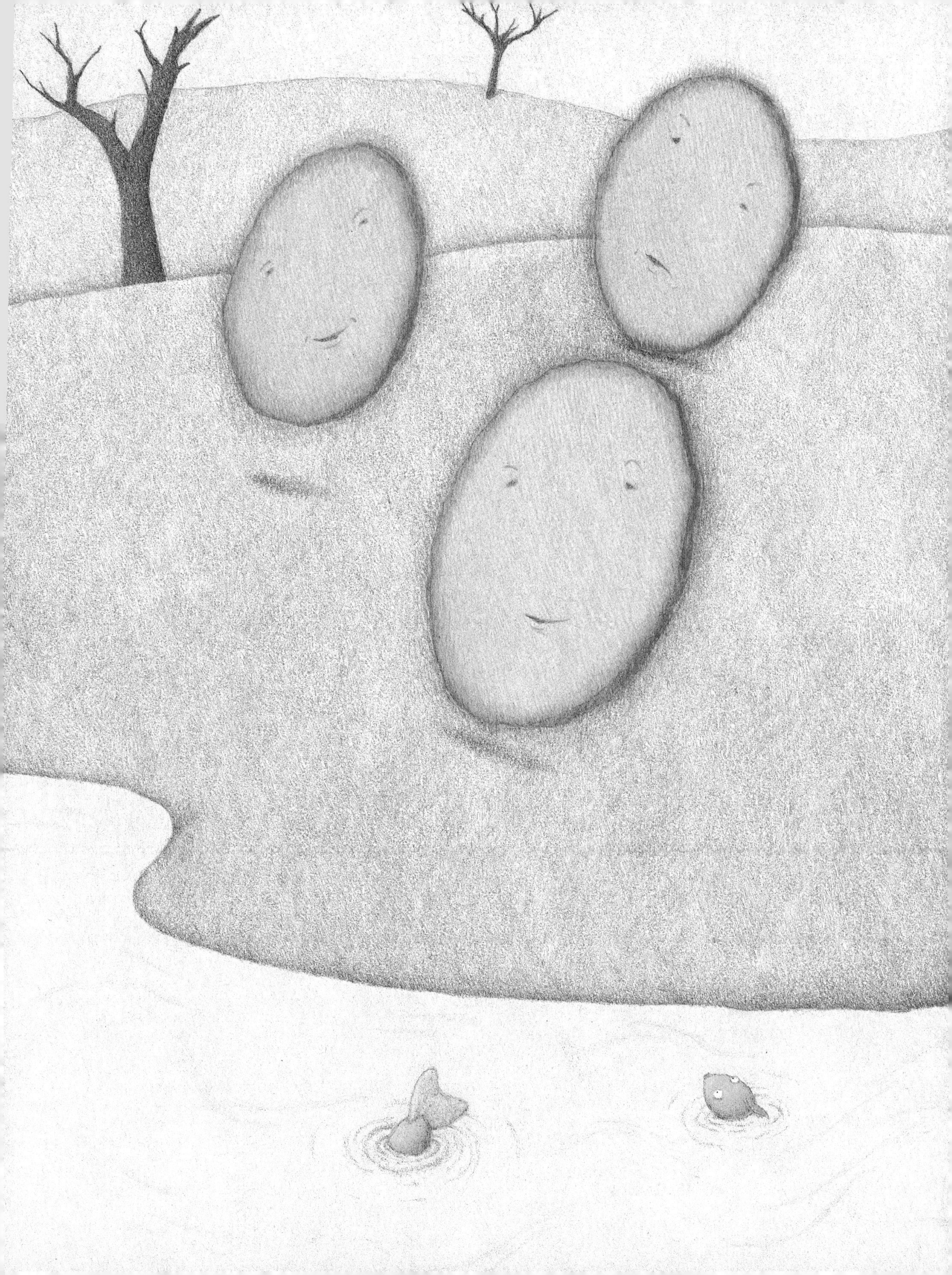

The latkes hadn't listened before, and they didn't listen now. But just as they plopped into the river—*kerplunk!*—a miracle happened. A modern-day Hanukkah miracle.

In front of everyone's eyes, the water in Applesauce River turned into *real applesauce*, the perfect bath for three crispy latkes.

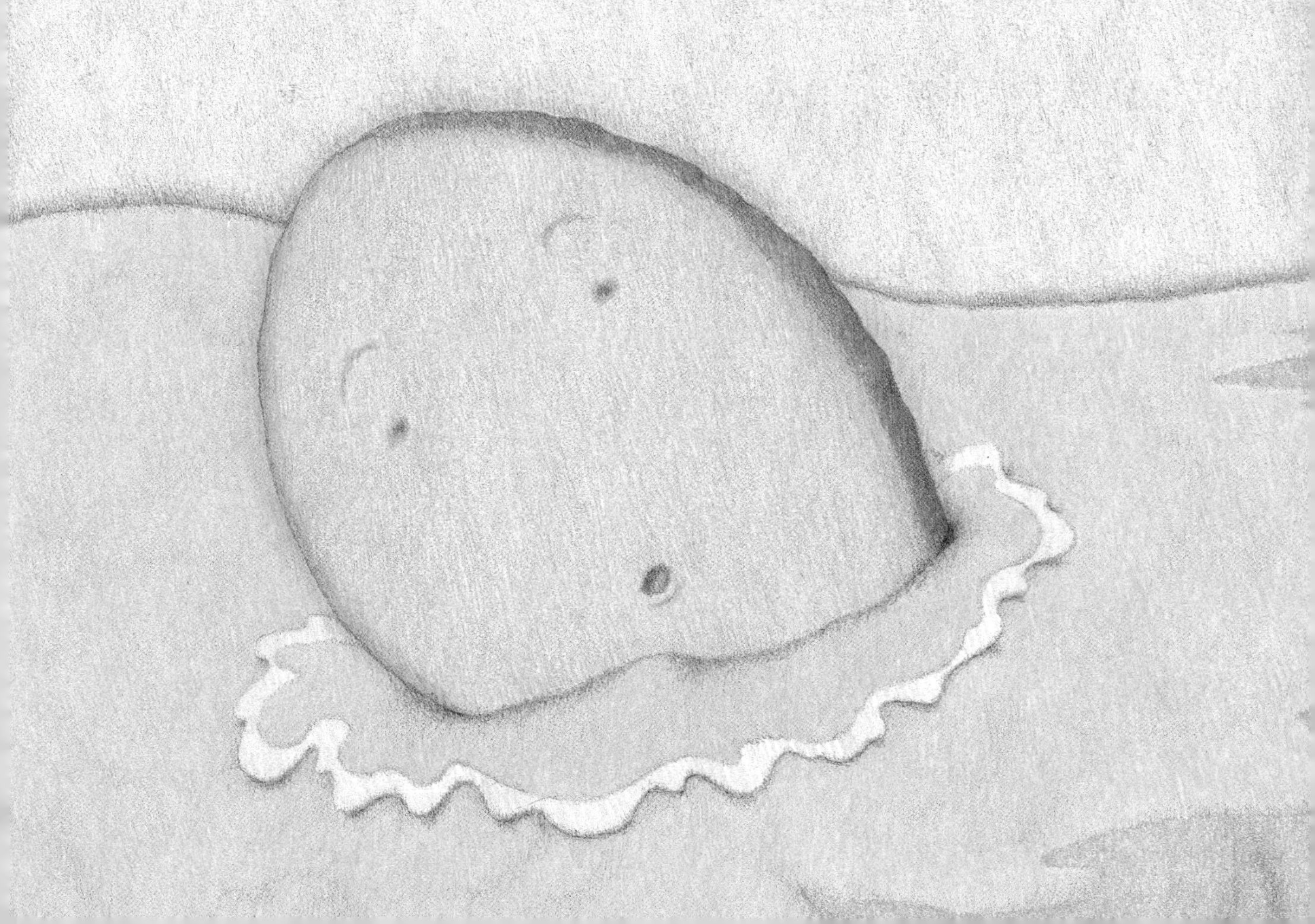

Rebecca blinked. Then one, two, three, she plucked the latkes right out of the river and put them on her tray. There were just enough latkes and just enough applesauce for each person to have one bite. Even after the pancakes' long trip through town, they tasted heavenly.

"Still, just one bite." The mayor sighed.

"I suppose one bite will have to do." Harry sighed. "And look! Applesauce River has turned back to water!"

"I wonder if I'll ever eat anything so delicious again." Sue sighed.

"Of course you will!" Rebecca answered her. "This very evening. You're all invited back to the synagogue for a Hanukkah celebration!"

Sure enough, at the synagogue that night Rebecca made certain there were plenty of latkes for the rabbi, the cantor, the boys, the mayor, Harry and Sue, and everyone else who came to the party. They lit the menorah, spun dreidels, danced, and noshed far into the night, singing:

Crisp and brown, big and round,
better latkes can't be found!

And they were right.

Mix together all the ingredients except the oil.
Heat the oil in a skillet until very hot.
To make each latke, drop a heaping tablespoon of the mixture
into the oil and flatten into a pancake shape.
Fry the latkes on one side; then turn and fry on the other.
Both sides should be crispy brown.
Drain the latkes on paper towels for a few minutes.
Serve with applesauce or sour cream. Serves 4–6.

If you are under 12, be sure to fry the latkes with a grownup's help!